IMPRINTS ON MY SOUL

JESSIE BESSIE & ME

DONALD D. CONLEY, SR.

Order this book online at www.trafford.com
or email orders@trafford.com

Most Trafford titles are also available at major online book retailers.

Print information available on the last page.

ISBN: 978-1-6987-0464-7 (sc)
ISBN: 978-1-6987-0463-0 (e)

Trafford rev. 11/24/2020

Trafford
PUBLISHING®   www.trafford.com
North America & international
toll-free: 844-688-6899 (USA & Canada)
fax: 812 355 4082

BESSIE

BY

DONALD D. CONLEY SR.

"BESSIE"

Habits, ideals and principals handed down from generation to generation can have catastrophic effects on a person's life in the years to follow. It's not a matter of finding fault or placing blame, this is about understanding why you are as you are.

BESSIE

Everyone knew her as Val, a smart but strange girl who lived in the small town of Bastrop La., with her Mother, two sisters and four brothers. My father had initially met her sister Eddie first, but Eddie was already involved with someone, so my father asked her if she had a sister. After being fair warned against the introduction, my father insisted. Eddie agreed and invited him to her home in Bastrop, La.

The day of the meeting, Val was home ironing. She kept their home impeccably neat and clean, never asking either of her two sisters or her mother Bessie to help. It was as if she had resigned herself as the sole house keeper, making certain that everything was in order. Almost like a compulsive disorder.

Bessie,(who made it no secret that she was entertaining three different men at the same time) was a feisty woman from what I'd been told in bits and pieces through the years. I only remember ever seeing her two times briefly in my entire life. I always felt as if we were being kept away from her deliberately by my mother.

BESSIE

Bessie had a brother known as "Son", as children we knew him as Uncle Son, who took a special liking to Val and he ultimately ended up having an intimate relationship with her starting at the age of 12, until the time of his death some forty years later.

Bessie had an entirely different prospective as far as Men. It was her belief that a woman had a responsibility to allow a man to be a man.

In her mind it was only natural for a man to act out his urges with the opposite sex, regardless of at whom that "urge" may be directed.

In the South back in those days, this was a subject that was widely known, but not ever spoken about in publics It was just accepted.

On the day of the meeting between my two parents (to be), my mother was in a section of the house ironing until Bessie appeared and ordered,

"Gal! You betta get in there an' sit with that man who come to see you'

Begrudgingly she complied.

BESSIE

At no point in that first meeting was there any semblance of the slightest interest on the part of Val, while my father on the other hand was determined to gain the trust of a woman who clearly demonstrates having no desire what so ever to even be civil. She was aloof and to the point throughout the entire time they spent in the parlor, accompanied by Eddie and her friend Gene.

It was a warm summer day as they all sat on opposite sides of the room, sipping lemonade. There was a cool breeze blowing through the entire house. Eddie and Gene sat laughing and talking together, while my father sat attempting to make conversation to no avail, until it was time to leave and he asked,

"Is it alright if I come and see you again?"

And she replied flatly,

"If that's what you feel like doing"

For whatever reason, my father continued to pursue my mother and subsequently ended up making a deathbed promise to her father," no matter what he would never leave her." My Mother over heard that promise

BESSIE

Shortly afterwards, my father took off for Chicago, vowing to send for my mother once he secured a job in the windy city. However, it was through the urging of Grand Ma Bessie that my mother followed my father via train and there they took up residence on the west side on Van Buren, in a basement apartment.

I must have been five years old when my father purchased a large brick home at 3240 west Walnut. All of the boys had a room to share, as did all of the girls, large enough for each one to have their own separate beds. There were two additional separate units. One my father rented out to an elderly couple, while the basement apartment was vacant most of the time.

It was the mid 1950's when Uncle Jimmy, my mother's brother came to Chicago to live with us. He was a round faced, always seemed jolly kind of a guy. But from the very first moment I met him, my first thought was that he looked absolutely nothing like my mother. Both their complexions were as different as night and day, not to mention facial similarities. There were absolutely none.

BESSIE

Jimmy was a Chef by trade as was my father, who secured a job for his brother in law at the same place where he worked in Palatine, Ill as a head chef. Jimmy's specialty was baking cakes and pastries.

Jimmy was all set. My father even allowed him to drive one of his numerous cars in order to get to work.

Inside of six months after moving to Chicago with his sister and brother in law, Jimmy was actively molesting three of his sisters six daughters.

His first victim was the youngest, who was easily sworn to secrecy.

Then, his second victim, the oldest daughter, who too kept silent

But his third victim ran and told her mother directly after he had his way with her only to be told,

"You stop that! An' you better not say anything to your daddy either!"

The child at the time was 9 years old. Jimmy would continue to have his way with the three girls for years under the same roof undetected by anyone else except Jimmy his sister.

BESSIE

The Twin Boys were born after the older brother
and sister. One twin was darker than the other
and clearly outweighed the lighter skin tone twin.
Preference was clearly shown from birth for the lighter
skin twin who was considered the more intelligent,
while the darker was felt to be more dominant.

Thus was the beginning of the "light
skin" coalition against the dark skin

I remember the very first time ever venturing
outside without the benefit of being carried
by one of my parents, or in a stroller. It was a
sunny day on the Westside of Chicago in 1956.
Although I was in the company of my father and
two brothers, they all walked ahead of me, both
my brothers holding on to my father's hand.

As we were crossing the street on the corner of
Lake Street and Homan ave. crossing under the
L Train commuter train tracks, suddenly an L
Train roared loudly directly above me. I froze in
the middle of the street, right in the middle of
traffic not knowing what that horrific loud noise
was, looking up until I heard my father yell,

"Donnie! Get out of the street boy!", causing me to
snap out of my daze and continue on across the street.

BESSIE

My two brothers stayed close to my father, each occasionally glancing back to sneer or make faces, not that it mattered to me since I did not feel as though I belonged with them anyway, but in the back and away was my place, by myself. I felt as if no one understood me and I made no attempts to be understood. I was going to be like Jessie Conley, My Grand —father whom my mother despised.

As the stories went, Jessie, who was killed before I was born, was known as a womanizer, feared by most men and a killer himself having served five years in Uma State Prison for killing his father in law, who promised to kill Jessie if he put his hands on his daughter again, who was Jessie's wife.

Jessie and his wife got into it. Jessie put hands on her. But instead of waiting for her father to come looking for him, Jessie went and sought him out; told him what he had done, an argument erupted. Jessie pulled a gun and shot his father in law to death.

BESSIE

A Crude Awakening

The old brick houses in Chicago all had steam heaters. I was born with Asthma and the humidity from the heat and steam made it hard for me to breathe. I was nine years old alone up in my room having a bad asthma attack. It was the dead of winter. Below zero conditions outside and I was trying to get outside in it.

I would dress only in a pair of summer short pants. T shirt and tennis shoes, go sit out on the front porch and I could breathe the cold air with ease. The neighbor's would see me as they passed by and would think that I had mental issues. And I probably did.(all associated with the bed wetting and bad school grades.)

My Aunt Eddie at that time, along with her husband uncle Gene and six children had stopped over on their way to California and were staying with us. At the same time my father was entering the front door, my aunt was entering the hallway from inside the house and just as I am about to yell, "Daddy help!" I froze at what I heard and saw.

BESSIE

Suddenly, without realizing it, I wasn't wheezing any more. Instead I was in shock at the sight of my father with tears streaming down his face, sniffling and whining as though he had been severely beaten by some force larger than he was. In his hand he held a paper saying,

"Look Eddie! Look what your sister did, had them people garnishee my check" My aunt replied

"Go in there an' beat her ass!"

"But Eddie, I can't do that!" he whined but my aunt said simply,

"l don't see why not. You go in there and beat her ass she won't do it no more"

I could not believe what I was seeing, let alone what I was hearing, but it was real. Although at that time I did not understand the reason as to what exactly it was that brought him to this pitiful state, I did know it was my mother who was the reason. From that point on I started to watch and study her.

With every year that passed, another new born was added to our rapidly growing brood, another reason to insure my father kept the promise he made to her father on his death bed to never leave her.

BESSIE

My mother had no consciousness of mind or shame when it came to her distain for dark comptexion people. I still can hear her say, "1 love to hear Nat King Cole sing, but I can't stand to look at him he's so black and ugly". Two of her own children who's skin color were darker than the rest of the children were clearly treated differently and more often than not, punished more severely than the others.

One of the darker skin children was a girl, the fifth child. She got pregnant at 15 and was sent away to a convent. Her child was given up for adoption. I was the first dark skin child birthed by my mother, born five minutes after my light complexion fraternal twin brother.

Unlike my twin brother, I wasn't interested in books and reading, or history and English. Truthfully speaking, I had absolutely no idea of what I wanted to be or do, other than to be as my mother cursed me to be, "Just like Jessie". I remember seeing a photograph of Jessie taken in the 1920's, when photography was relatively new. He looked like a black man with a thick mustache.

BESSIE

My mother absolutely despised my grand-
father and more often than not she would jeer
and taunt me with what she thought were slurs
about me being like my grand-father.

"You gone be just like that damn ole
Jessie. You ain't gone be no good"

I never really understood exactly why she was
so resentful towards him although one thing I
did know for certain was that she hated the man
and it made me want to be exactly like him.

From the time of my birth, my siblings and I
were raised in a Cult-like fashion. We were
not allowed to socialize with the other kids in
the neighborhood because, they went to Public
School and we attended Catholic school which
was a block further away from our house.

I did not understand the power my mother held over
my father. He was the one who went to work every
day, sometimes holding down two jobs, along with
a side hustle or two at the pool hall. While the only
thing my mother did was lay around barking orders,
sopping biscuits and syrup all day. Then when my
father got home after work, she would go into her act,

"1 been slaving around this house all day an' I can't get these kids to do nothing, especially that Donald" and the next sound I'd hear was his voice commanding, "Donnie! Get in here". Never asking to hear my side of any allegation against me, only informing me that I am about to be punished.

Unlike my twin brother, my school grades were not that impressive, yet I was always being compared to him as he being a better example of us both,

"Why don't you go up stairs and read a book like your brother?"

"Because I'm not like my brother" I would speak to myself silently, but not ever aloud.

One thing about my mother was that she made it known exactly who her favorites were and if you weren't considered one of them, it was best that you kept your distance and not bring too much attention to yourself. She always seemed in a bad mood, or at least that was my perception.

BESSIE

I can recall countless times throughout the years
when a cousin, or a friend of my father would
stop by our house, my father would formally
introduce his three sons, starting with the oldest,

"Now, this is my oldest, this is Raymond.
He's going grow up to own his own mechanic
shop, cause that's what he likes to do."

Then my father would introduce the next in line,

"This is Ronald, he's going to be a priest or a Doctor
when he grows up because, he's is a heavy thinker."

When it came my turn to be introduced
my father would simply say,

"This is Donald, but we don't want to talk about
that" and disburse with the introductions.

One October evening in 1959 Raymond
and I were up in our room.

I was on the top bunk, while Raymond had a bed
of his own on the other side of the room. He said,

"Man, I was thinking everybody at school from the fifth grade to the 8th got to write with a fountain pen. Them things are ten dollars! But if we had a bunch of um, we could sell um at the school for two dollars easy"

"Let's go!" was all I said and together he and I headed out for Goldblats, a Department store on the Westside of Chicago. I was dressed in a light jacket and catholic school uniform with tie, while my brother chose to dress in in a heavy winter coat.

Once we arrived at the store, I immediately separate myself from him because I already know how clumsy he is. Always making certain that he stays at least an isle away from me, chances are the store security will be busy watching Raymond.

After a few minutes and having felt satisfied, it was time to go. I motion to Raymond to go.

BESSIE

I am fifteen to twenty feet behind Raymond as he is headed towards the exit door of the department store. Directly behind him appeared a store security person, a white man in plain clothes who grabs Raymond by the back of his collar and the seat of his pants, ripping them in the process.

He drags my brother off somewhere I don't know, but I just keep walking right on out of the store and the moment I stepped passed the door, I struck out running. I got away. First I made it around to the alley and back of the store, where I hid my loot under a garbage can. I walk back into the store and spot a Floor Walker. I walk up to him and say, "Excuse me sir, but I'm looking for my brother" a middle age white man

"is that right" he replies taking hold of my arm "as a matter of fact I was just looking for you".

Immediately I pretend not to know what this is about, only providing enough resistance so as to appear confused.

Once stepping into the office, I first notice another balding white man sitting behind a desk with a mountain of fountain pens and Raymond sitting in a chair in front of the desk slobbering with tears in his eyes.

The detective who escorted me into the office instructed me to empty my pockets and without hesitation I did as I was told. I had only some change and a pocket knife, which I sat on the desk before him. He asked "Where's yours?"

"My what?" I replied but he insisted,

"Come on I know you got some too" glancing with a smirk at Raymond.

But I was adamant,

"l don't know what you talking about. I ain't took nothing and can't nobody say they saw me take nothin!

"Well", he spoke slowly, "Since this is your first time, I'm going to have to call your parents-" instantly Raymond starts wailing!

"Oh no mister please! Please don't call my daddy; he close to seven feet tall and he gone kill me"-l cut him off,

"Stop it Raymond! Too late for that, now tell him what he want to know and let's get out of here!"

"Oh!, so you're the smart one" the white man
behind the desk remarked at me, "Come on
tell me, what you do with your load".

I maintained my position as Raymond gave
the other detective our phone number. After a
few rings, my mother answered the phone by
identifying herself after the man explained who
he was and why he was calling. He said,

"I'm calling from down here at Goldblatt's
Department store and I have two of your son's
here, both caught stealing-I' I immediately started
to yell loudly enough so my mother could hear,

"Oh no you didn't! You didn't catch me
stealing nothin!" causing the man on
the phone to clarify his statement,

"Ah, that is, we only caught the oldest one stealing. We
didn't find any of the stolen items on the other one, so
as a first time courtesy I am calling you, but your son is
not allowed to step into the store again." In my mind I
had managed to elude not one punishment, but two.

After leaving the store and making our way back
to our house, that is, after I ran to the alley and
retrieved my loot I was in a real good mood.

Throughout the entire journey back to 3240 west walnut I taunted and antagonized my older brother with words of doom, bloody and severe punishment administered by the man he feared most in life, the man known to have been a hero on a navy war ship in world war two, a man who above all else believed in the law, in fact, he even had a part time job working as a correction officer in Joliet State Prison.

By the time Raymond and I made it in from the store fiasco, my father still had not come in from work. We were met at the front door by mother, who directed us both to go to our room. I remember Ronald being in the room on the bottom bunk as I climbed up on top and began to empty packs of fountain pens from my socks, pockets my

waist band, inside my tucked shirt and the sleeves of my jacket. I had a mound of pens on my bed, as Raymond lay face down on his bed dreading the sound of the front door opening announcing Daddy is home.

Short and sweet, had it been me alone, I would have been beaten nearly to death, but my mother never said a word to my father.

Finding My Place

Modern studies have shown that life has different effects on children who are raised in the same environment with both parents about as equally as children raised in a broken home without the benefit of having two parents. A Dysfunctional family setting clearly leaves a very nasty emotional scar. However, the bottom line is Choices. We all have the ability to choose.

Weak Strong Good Bad all are choices we make with our lives. People only do what they know.

Between School during the week Chores on Saturday, church on Sunday I had no sense of mind other than to wait for directions. Aside of that my only aspiration was to be like my Grand-Father, whom my mother so vehemently despised. I had only heard storied about him in bits and pieces, of how ruthless and cold he was. Men feared him and women adored him. Jessie became my Role Model and Idol.

It was common practice back in the days of Black and White TV, if you

"Spare the Rod, you Spoil the Child", something today that would be considered as Criminal Child Abuse. I learned at an early age how to avoid the wrath of my mother who would easily become enraged, especially with me.

I had issues with bed wetting that led to at least three beatings by my mother each week because my mother didn't like having to wash the sheets and bed clothes.

That episode of my life passed when after being laughed at one morning by my brothers about the bed wetting, I decided that I was not going to walk with them to school. Instead I would walk alone, but I would go the way they were afraid to go. Past Jacob Beidler public school.

Most of the boys at the public school had served stints at St. Charles reformatory and were known to carry switch blade knives. As walked alone there were a couple of guys who seemed to be eying me, but I kept walking.

The next day instead of walking to school with my brothers, again I

chose to walk the short way, past Beidler. This time there was a group of three girls, all clearly in their early teens who began to encircle me, one taking my book bag as the other two hook their arms to mine and escorted me the rest of the way to St. Matthews.

I was young with curly hair and they made me their Mascot. They let the boys at the school know that I was not to be bothered in any way. As it turned out these girls where actually called Lady Vice Lords, the female version of the male gang. Every day I would go that way alone and my brothers thought I was crazy and I made no effort to tell them about my new found friends.

After a few weeks of taking that route every morning without my brothers and sister, the bed wetting stopped and I noticed how much differently my siblings were reacting towards me. Especially Raymond who asked,

"Ain't you scared those public school
kids gone jump you?"

I simply pulled out my pocket knife and
quickly opened it with my thumb and said,

"Nope", closed it with one hand and
put it back in my pocket.

The first four born were all given a weekly allowance because they maintained good school grades. The only "allowance" I ever saw came from the public school girls and my pop bottle return hustle, which was how I had money for the movies and back then was only 20 cents.

The messages and situations I was experiencing within the circle called family, clearly had a monumental effect on my life. The main lessons I learned about Life were through watching my mother and father.

Only now do I realize that they were doing what they knew. There were no guide lines, or parenting formats to follow other than, "Spare the rod.

Spoil the child"

There were things that I did not understand, but had no other choice but to accept. Even what I felt wasn't right, I still had to accept it or face punishment. I knew at an early age not to complain, or risk a brutal admonishment for having the audacity to think that I had any rights.

My father always cut the boys hair and when he was done with me, the back of my neck would always be cut and bleeding from his lining the back of my head with clippers that were too sharp, but not once did I ever complain. I just sat there and took it because, in my mind, this is the way a Man acts.

The only thing that stuck with me, were the negative aspects of my life.

Since there was absolutely nothing or anyone to show me anything different that is, until Aunt Della came to town.

It was around the spring of 1962 when my Father announced his Sister was coming to visit on her

way to California, so without saying anything
else, we all understood to be on our best behavior.
This would be the first time I ever even had
the inclination that my Father had a sister.

The sun was shining brightly that day Aunt Della
came to visit. There was an entourage of three yellow
cabs, two were specifically for her luggage, while she
rode in the front cab, just as the Queen of England
is chauffeured in her private limo.(s) and carriages.

The driver rushed around to open the back passenger
door for his passenger, as the moment Aunt Della
stepped from the back door of the cab, a symphony
seemed to go off in my head, as everything around
me seemed to start moving in Slow motion.

She was draped in a waist length fur jacket. Diamond
and gold bracelets on both her wrist along with
a diamond broach around her neck. She and my
father even looked like they were related, except
for her fair complexion and beautiful green eyes.

It was like Royalty had come to our house, so of
course my father had to go through his ritual, except
this time all the girls were in line too according
to their age. Something almost magical happened
to me that day when my Father had gotten to
me, the forth in line. As he attempted to dismiss
me, Aunt Della spoke up to my Father saying,

"Wait a minute. Hold it!" she commanded in her
soft song like voice holding up her right hand as
she knelt down in front of me, placing both of her
hands gently to my face, then kissed me softly,

"You stop saying things like that
Ed!" then she spoke to me,

"You gonna be just fine, you hear me?" smiling
warmly as she held me close to her while my Father
continued on with introducing his children.

For the first time in my life I felt love.

I will forever remember being amazed. Stunned to
the point of feeling in a daze about Aunt Della. She
stayed with us for a couple of weeks. My Father gave
her the basement apartment, which too had front
door access. It was spacious and contained everything.
Furniture, kitchen appliances. She was comfortable
and I made it a point to be at her every beck and call.

Aunt Della stayed with us for a couple of weeks. All of
my siblings were making their best attempts at getting
her attention, but she had made her choice clear. I
was on a cloud happy! I felt a real sense of love and
affection from another human-being. Unknowingly,
I had slowly begun to emotionally distance myself
from my mother, not that she would of noticed,
since I felt virtually invisible in her eyes anyway.

It was a very sad day for me when Aunt Della had to continue her trip out west. I maintained my composure, although inside it was another story. I wanted to say "Take me with you!", but instead I just stood silently when she placed her arm around me to walk her down the steps to another fleet of yellow cabs.

BESSIE

My Father walked beside my Mother, who was caring my youngest sister, the rest of the family behind them. Aunt Della and I in front when my Father stated that we were all driving to the train station.

There wasn't even a conversation about it, I just automatically got in the cab with her and rode to the station. Aunt Della and my Father spoke privately as the Red Caps began to unload the taxi cabs. Aunt Della said brief good-byes to all my brothers and sisters, but when she got to me, she leaned over, kissed me and said,

"Don't you let nobody tell you what you can't do. You put your mind to it and you can do anything you want to do, so long as it's right in the eyes of God", she kissed me as she held my face in her hands,

"You'll do just fine." She stood up and waved good-bye to the family boarded the train and was gone.

SUMMER 1962

I can honestly say that even though meeting my Aunt Della changed my opinion of women, where I naturally figured all women are wicked and manipulative, all arrived from watching my Mother, I still maintained a watchful eye on her every word and move. I was studying her.

My Mother was known to have a "Bad Disposition" (to say the least) while her Sister-ln-Law was the complete opposite. Why couldn't Aunt Della be my Mother, I would think to myself. I felt as if my Mother was a direct punishment from God and I had to endure it. I guess it was that Catholic indoctrination of having to suffer like Job did.

I was virtually taught from birth that camaraderie was none existence within our house, at least to only a chosen few. I accepted my position without comment or emotion. Pain was inevitable, while suffering was optional and I chose not to suffer. During my entire adolescent life my Father always cut the boys hair first and always starting with Raymond, then Ronald and lastly by the time it was my turn, the back of my neck would be scarred and bloody from the clippers being too sharp, yet I would not ever flinch with pain or show any signs of any.

I had it locked in my mind that no matter what, I would not ever show signs of weakness to anyone. My attitude was slowly growing hostile within the confines of my surroundings, yet I remained respectful and did my best to go along with the flow of things. Both at school and in the house. But things didn't always turn out uneventful on Walnut St.

All of the siblings born within my age group seemed to always test me. There was a time when one of their pranks back fired on them. What was thought would send me into a panic, actually caused me to be more relaxed. A few days earlier, my brother found the family cat dead in the basement. "Mickey", apparently had choked itself to death by getting its head stuck in a milk crate.

The ploy was that l, along with my two brothers and three sisters would all go down in the basement to take care of the dead cat in the milk crate. They were all acting so afraid, but the instructions to go in the basement came from my mother, so it had to be done and before Daddy came from work. Not being of the same mindset, I opened the basement door and flipped on the light switch. As I headed down the stairs

I took maybe five, six steps down into the basement when suddenly Wham! I hear the door behind me slam shut. Suddenly there was total darkness the light goes out from the switch on the other side of the door. I stopped on the seventh step. My sense of hearing became acute. My senses were suddenly alive. I could hear my siblings laughing and snickering behind the door.

I casually take a seat there on the step
and become one with my senses

I can hear them as their laughter gets louder while I sit there in silence taking in everything around me. Even though I could not see my hand in front of my face, still I felt no need to panic. Maybe five minutes passed before the door cracked open, but I yelled

"Close the door!"

I had taken away their reason; their purpose showing them that it meant absolutely nothing to mea I had taught myself how to interact with my sisters and brothers, at the same time teaching them who:

was which was not one of them.

This divide and conquer mentality was implemented by my mother early on in my life, something that allowed her to maintain total control over everyone, including my Father. Meaning, on numerous occasions she would make clear announcements when a delivery was made to the house while my Father was at work.

"And none of you better not tell your Daddy", once she had hidden whatever it was down in the basement, knowing that the chances of him going down there after working were slim to none. I mean big tag items like washing machines and dryers, furniture you name it. She was spending money as fast as he could make it, like she was married to an oil Barron and what she wasn't spending she was hoarding.

My oldest brother, as a result of being the first born in our house, was clearly placed in a category all his own by my parents, although he was not exactly the sharpest crayon in the box. His grades were average but outside of that he displayed no special talents or creativity.

He had made the Alter Boy list. Played football in high school, but had a better performance record holding the communion plate, then he did at scoring a touchdown. He was coddled and praised for the dumbest and insignificant things.

But, he was the first born baby boy, who in my mind was scared of his own shadow and super stupid. As a result of having to share a bedroom with him and my twin, plus seeing him interact at school with the other students, I felt as if I knew him better than he knew himself. He was for the most part a hypochondriac.

If he wanted to get out of anything, all he had to do was say he didn't feel good and that was all it took for my mother to send him back to bed. There were times like any normal twelve year old he would experience a slight cough, which more than likely derived from his sneaking to smoke cigarettes in the boys rest room at school.

Never the less, my Mother told my Father that it was a bad case of asthma. The Chicago weather was not good for him and she told my Father that he needed to send Raymond to California to live with his Aunt Della.

I have to admit I was mentally paralyzed at the news that he was being sent to California to live where I wanted to be. With Aunt Della He was gone in the following two weeks. There was no fan fair send off when he left. Truth is, I really don't how if he went by plane or train since

My Father drove him to his mode
of travel with no one else.

It would be another year before we would see our oldest brother again. Even though during his time out west, the only person who maintained regular phone calls to Raymond was my mother I believe was her way of getting regular reports on how life was compared to being in Chicago. I feel as if it was at that time when she decided to hatch the plan to uproot the whole house

With the oldest of our Brood away, it felt like the entire dynamics of life around the house changed. Personally, the only aspect of his absence that I found disturbing was how he ended up where I wanted to be.

In that year Raymond was in California, I found total acceptance among the public school students. The girl crew that chose me as their mascot made the introductions, more so to promote camaraderie between us when they were not around.

BESSIE

I didn't attempt to approach any of the girls at my own school because, I felt as though I was out of my "league" (so to speak), not that I was even entertaining the idea of becoming intimate with my lady friends because, I had absolutely no interest in sex. But all of the girls at my own school were so smart, while even in school I was not one of the "In Crowd", maybe not in the house I wasn't, but in the neighborhood I was acknowledged.

It was during those years when I started noticing the difference in people, as far as being prejudice. My Mother use to say,

"1 love to hear Nat King Cole sing but I can't stand to look at him he's so black and ugly/'

At first I thought she was trying to be funny, but I soon realized that this was her outright disdain being voiced out loud, her utter disgust for people with dark skin. In my mind I didn't know how to articulate or assimilate what to surmise from it, but I did know it was not good.

BESSSIE

That whole year felt odd. As I look back on it now, it could have very been that everyone knew about the move to California except me and no one made any attempt to tell me. I was too busy with experiencing something other than what was being presented to me. I was getting to know people who lived in a world that was far different from mine.

These people accepted me without judgement or criticism, while my twin brother and three sisters had started to believe I was different and they began to keep their distance. There were times when out of the blue my mother would lecture me on not associating with the public school kids, which let me know that my brother and sisters were not only watching me, but they were telling on me to our mother,

A Reflection

There was one other time our entire household, with
the exception of my Father left Chicago, driven by an
Uncle, the brother of my mother. My Father had to
work, so Jimmy was the designated driver, since my
mother did not know how to drive. The visit to see
Grand Ma Bessie is so vague, until I can only recall
seeing her one time throughout the whole time there.

It was a swelteringly hot that day in Bastrop,
La. My Mother had told my twin brother and I
to go in the room and take a nap. We went in
the room as instructed, but instead of taking a
nap I was down on the floor with a big red ball,
kicking it to Ronald who sat on the bed kicking
it back, plus too, just in case Mother should look
in the room, he could play like he was asleep.

I had kicked the ball to Ronald just as this old guy with
white hair and beard appeared at the open window.
He spoke clearly as he leaned in the window,

"How you boys doin?", then proceeded to climb
all the way inside the window and took a seat
there on the window ledge continuing as he
looked down at me where I sat on the floor,

"What's your name"

"Donald" I replied looking up into his hazel green eyes. He turned to my brother seated on the side of the bed and asked the same question. He then sat silently for what seemed like a long time just smiling and sort of gazing first from my brother, then to me. I kicked the ball to him as he sat on the ledge and he kicked it back to Ronald, then it was on.

It may have lasted maybe two, three minutes before he announced,

"Well, I got to be goin' now. But ya'll be good" then he climbed out the same way he came in. Seconds later, Grand Ma Bessie with my Mother directly behind her burst through the door. My Mother screaming,

"l thought I told ya'll to take a nap. I heard ya'll talking, who else was in

I replied, "Gran-Pa Fred", in that instant Grand-Ma Bessie collapsed like a sack of potatoes on to the floor. She fainted.

Years later I would learn that the reason why she fainted was because Grand Pa Fred had been dead since the year we were born.

A few days later we were back in the station wagon loaded up in route for Chicago, when my uncle fell asleep at the wheel and ran straight into a telephone pole in Little Rock Arkansas. The car was totaled. We were all driven to a local hospital and provided with our own private room. The doctors and nurses acted as though a politician or some type of royalty had been admitted to their small out of the way hospital.

One of my sisters broke her arm, while everyone else was mostly shook up. I think Jimmy got cut on the forehead by glass, but other than that, it was all good. My Father had to provide train accommodations for six children and two adults. I'm not certain if he had to pay for that telephone pole Jimmy took out and then too there was the hospital bill

It wasn't long after the car accident and we were all back in Chicago when, "Pack up what you want to take with you. Leave the rest we're moving to California"

All of a sudden I was stunned. No! Wait! What do I do? I've got to let the friends I made at the public school know that I won't be around.

Time after that point began to move in a whirl pool, like Dorothy in the Wizard of Oz, she was hit on the head and the whole house was caught up in the whirl wind only to land on the sister of a wicked witch.

But this was not Kansas it was Chicago and it wasn't Oz, but California where we were headed. I may have stood frozen for a second or two as I watched my brothers and sisters run about the house with joy and excitement about moving, while I stood stuck wondering if this would be a good time to run away because I did not want to leave my friends.

I sat in the back of the filled to capacity green and white 1959 dodge Station wagon as my Father drove us to the train station. All of my siblings were laughing and excited about moving out west, while for me I wanted no part of it. At the Station I heard my Father tell my Mother that he would meet us there as soon as he sold the house and finished other business matters.

It took all of three days to get to California. Aunt Della and Raymond were there to meet us at the Station. I don't know about everybody else, but I was so glad to see Aunt Della that I ran straight to her, while everybody else ran to Raymond. My mother followed behind holding the youngest. "Hi Son" Aunt Della's voice sang to me as I wrapped my arms around her. "Hi Auntee" I said probably grinning like a "Chest Cat"

She drove a white four door 1958 Chevy Impala. As we made our way to the parking lot, I met Uncle Clay, Aunt Della's husband a Painter by trade. He had to drive his car too, a 1951 Chevy that the steering wheel would come completely off the column. But he was only trying to spook everybody.

Uncle Clay stood around five foot nine, was brown complexion and a good natured guy for the most part. He and Aunt Della had no children and I just figured they didn't want any of their own. But between the two of them, I found myself spending more time at their home than I did at my own house.

After a few weeks of being in our first house in Berkeley, my Mother decided that she did not like the house and instructed my Father to send her more money so she could find another house and obediently my Father complied.

Only with the assistance of Aunt Della, my Mother acquired another house in North Oakland on 38 th street between Telegraph and

Webster. Neatly kept lawns and freshly painted homes along the entire block. Vibrant green trees up and down the pristine street, yet one block away presides one of the most notorious boulevards known for Prostitution. Mac Author Boulevard.

This was the section of North Oakland where one would go in order to see the latest fashion and expensively customized Cadillacs and Lincoln Continentals. The streets lined with ladies of the night, all dressed in after six gowns and dresses, while The prospective customers cruise up and down the boulevard searching for the right one to lose their soul.

1965. The year when the Temptations
came out with their big hit

"My Girl" My father was still back in Chicago
settling his affairs and it wasn't like I was running
wild. But I was growing into My Own without the
benefit of direction. At the age of 15, I remember
my first life lesson outside of the classroom.

Her name was Judy. A slim pretty brown
skin 29 year old sporting lady sitting out on
the front porch of the duplex next door to
our house on 38th street when I hear,

"Hey ole pretty brown skin boy!"

I look up where the sound came from at the top step
of the porch next door, I see a woman in her night
gown, cigarette in one hand, cup of coffee in the
other and for the first time in my life in clear view
under her night gown her panty-less bottom.

I remember telling myself to look directly in her eyes.

"Come on up here and talk to me" she invited and
without hesitation I climbed the steps to take a seat
next to her. I introduced myself and at that instant we
became friends. More so, she became my Mentor.

From that day on it seemed like my life would not ever be the same. It was like destiny was developing its course in my life and I knew only but to follow it. Judy and I would sit and talk for hours there on the front porch. As my brothers and sisters would arrive at our house from school, they would see me talking with Judy and I would introduce them as they passed on into the house, thus my Mother being apprised of my activity.

Looking back on my life: the basic influence to shape my character has been a woman, while the male figure in my life was not as dominant as I felt it should have been Never the less, it wasn't long after before I met Johnny Paul, the man who Judy claimed as her Pimp. He drove a red convertible Cadillac Coupe De Ville that Judy proudly boasted about having bought.

During one of our many front porch conversations, she told me the story about Abraham and Sarah from the Bible, how they had to flee from Jerusalem into Egypt but Abraham told her to say that she was his sister out of fear that these other rulers would attempt to kill him in order to get to Sarah if they knew she was his wife.

While in Egypt Abraham met a king, who invited both Abraham and Sarah to stay at his palace as his guest That night in a dream an Angel had come to him to tell him that Sarah was not the sister, but a the wife of Abraham, which was considered as a violation of their laws, that required the offender to compensate the offended husband.

The King paid Abraham in a vast amount of land, sheep and goats to redeem himself for his violation of the sacred law. Judy then made the reference to Abraham as being the first Pimp. She would say everything she was sharing with me is not taught in school because, that is one of the white man's fears is for a Black Man to find out who he really is. She spoke so knowledgably and I hung on to every word.

Life around me was starting to take shape. Although I had absolutely no desire to become a pimp, I found the information provided by my well season sporting lady next door neighbor to be priceless. Her motto was "Get the money first because, romance without finance is a nuisance", which made sense to me, especially being that I did not have the first clue as to what to do during the act of having sex. The only vagina I had ever seen in my life was that day I looked up the steps at Judy.

The summer of 1965, in Oakland was a time when political awareness was becoming a forefront in the news. Starting with the killing of an unarmed Black youth by Oakland police officers Bobby Hutton and I were not only in the same grade at Woodrow Wilson Jr. High, but we also got summer jobs with the Neighborhood Youth Core on 55th and Market in North Oakland. Bobby Seal was our counselor.

It was 1967 when the Oakland police murdered Bobby Hutton in cold blood. The police claimed to be investigating some sort of tip and ordered the occupants inside to come out with their hands in the air. Bobby

Hutton was the first to come out shirtless and with both hands in the air. As he is all the way out on the porch and clearly visible, some officer yelled, "Gun!", and seventeen year old Bobby Hutton was riddled with bullets by the hands of the Oakland police.

By the time my Father had made it to California after concluding his business back in Chicago, I was pretty much on the road to perdition. One day my twin brother and I were having a fight in the house when my Father appeared from nowhere and kneed me in the head knocking me off of my brother

I quickly recover and jump to my feet cursing, "Mutha-Fucka! What you kick me for" "Boy what you say!" my father asked calmly "You heard me!" I retorted in anger

"I think you better step into the back yard"

The instant after I said it I knew it was too late to back down, so I continue on with the role,

"Then come on! I ain't scared" and stormed out of the back door to the back yard. The truth be known, I was about to eliminate on myself I was so scared. I stepped into the middle of the yard and turned around to square off as my Father came sauntering out of the back door with all of my brothers and sisters following him.

Another fine mess you've gotten me into, I remember thinking from the comedy team of Stanley Laurel and Oliver Hardy. As he got closer to me he didn't even put his hands up, but just led with a right cross and caught me square in the chest, dazing me, but I stayed on my feet.

There was a moment when I had a shot but hesitated and he caught me again except that time I saw stars letting me know that one more shot like that and lights out. It suddenly occurred to me that he recently had a Hernia operation, so when he went to lead with his right, I ducked, stepped into him and hit him with a hard right hand directly where he had been cut open and he dropped to one knee.

At first my mother was yelling, "That's right kill him Ed", but the moment I dropped him she started screaming for the police and I took off running. I stayed away from the house for the next three days. It wasn't even in my mind to finish him. He was my Father and I really did not want to fight him.

That day when I did finally go back, it was early evening and he was sitting alone down stairs with nothing but the light from the TV news. I could hear the rest of the people in the house moving around upstairs as I stepped through the door to see him there in the dark. He spoke calmly,

"Hey boy, come on in here" I'm thinking to myself, if he wants to have a round two I'm getting off first this time. Cautiously I approach closer and he says, "Have a seat. You eat yet?" I take a seat in the straight chair next to his recliner, watching his hands all the while.

"I'm not hungry" I answered watching him as he not once took his eyes off the television. There was a moment of silence to pass between us, he finally spoke again saying slowly,

"Listen. You know you're a man now. And the next time we have a disagreement, I'm gonna get my gun and I'm gonna shoot you". The only thing I said in response was "Ok". Three days later I had moved out and did not go back.

Once my Father made his position clear as to what he would do at our next disagreement, it rang loud and clear in my mind. I knew that there would be a "next time", so I knew too there wasn't any need in parlaying the inevitable. I got out of there, After all, my Father told me I was a man now.

I had been verbally emancipated by my Father, yet I still had the need to show him that I was just as good as my brothers. I remember the first thing he said when he saw my new Cadillac convertible when I was only nineteen years old,

"Boy", them police gone kill you".

JESSIE

BY

DONALD D. CONLEY SR.

JESSIE

by

Ronald De Collier Sr.

THE REAL SECRET

Jachim and Anne were married giving birth
to a daughter whom they name Mary, since
the child had been conceived before the two
had wed. The name meaning, "Bitter".

As the years passed the child grew into womanhood.
Politics began to emerge and Dictatorship was
taking over the country. The people living in small
towns and villages did not want to upset the new
and powerful regime of the Roman Empire.

Roman soldiers enter their town and a soldier by
the name of Pantera (which means black) he see's
Mary and rapes her, but when she tells her parents
they tell her to keep quiet about it, so not to create
trouble with the new Roman government. Her
parents said it was an "Immaculate Conception"

Clearly, what is done in the dark, will
eventually come to the light...

JESSIE

"If I only knew then what I know now". The truth be told, looking back on my life I realize I was attempting to commit suicide by police with acting like "Jessie". Willfully Ignorant or Psychologically, Emotionally and mentally under developed. I only knew what I did not want, a trend of thought that I am now conscious of.

I'm sure there are many Men who would gladly trade places to have women eager, willing and able to provide virtually anything needed to live comfortably. That would not be a problem for me as long as I had mutual feelings for the woman. That is where it gets complicated for me. I do not consider myself a selfish person and I make it a point to always be fair with people.

I have always felt that fair exchange is no robbery and I know not to bite the hand that feeds me. In life I have learned through experience that you always end up the way you start out. Start out lying in a new relationship and you will end up always lying in that relationship.

"We choose our joys and sorrows long before we experience them", is what Kahil Kabran wrote, which I interpret as the choices me make at the start of anything in our life that becomes a fixture or essential part.

Like when my Aunt advised my Father against becoming involved with who turned out to be my mother. He faced opposition at virtually every turn of that marriage until he initiated divorce proceedings thirty years later.

I know my Father took a certain pride in having his own family and he stuck it out for thirty-years for reasons that I will not ever understand.

That was something I would not subject myself to for thirty Days!

One man's pride is another man's punishment. All as a result of the Choice Initially made.

I went to state prison for eleven counts of armed robbery and three counts of bank robbery when I was 19 years old. Newly sentenced prisoners were sent to the receiving and intake center located in Vacaville, California. One day while walking through the corridor, this prisoner on a work detail, accompanied by a guard, had dropped a box filled with typing paper that flew everywhere.

As I was passing by the guard ordered me to stop and help pick up the papers. I refused because I was not assigned to the Detail, which the JESSIE

Guard viewed as refusing a Direct Order, while other prisoners passing complied without question. The Duce's were pressed on the guards short wave radio, within minutes The Goon Squad show up in full force to swiftly place me in handcuffs and escort me to the disciplinary Lt's office.

After waiting for the hallway guard to forward the write-up, the guard appears and conveys his version of what happened personally inside the private office. When I am directed to step into the office and take a seat. The prison uniform was too small for the fat white man sitting behind the desk was the first thing I noticed, as he started with,

You gone have to learn son to do what you're told by an officer. But I was of another mindset. I had read the rule book that stated no newly sentenced prisoner will be required to work on any detail unless he is assigned to the kitchen or laundry. I wasn't assigned to either other than tests from physicals to IQ's.

I quoted the rule book. I could see in his eyes he felt challenged while clearly I was in no position to even think such a thing, yet I did and I was within my miniscule prison rights. He went on." I see here at your last

Classification hearing you were put in for Soledad, but Son I can tell you with that attitude you're not

gonna make it." I remember thinking to myself,
yeah, and neither is that shirt you got on fat bastard.

Just turning Twenty years of age at Soledad State prison
in the mid 1970's was a political awareness era, when
practically everywhere you looked out on the streets,
especially Oakland, there was a poster or a sign reading
"Free" Somebody. But there was another dark culture
brooding with the misguided and directionless.

People with no hope of being any more than
what they already were found guilty to be as on
most days racial tension was high between the
three dominate races. The Brothers The Mexicans
and the Whites. One word made the difference
if you lived or died at the hands of another.

Respect.

My attitude was that whatever the politics were going
on outside my jail cell had nothing to do with me, since
there was only one number behind my name, which
meant I was not "Buddy Hustling" and the only thing
I required was Fifty-Feet, which meant Stay Away.

I absorbed myself in learning how to type and
strengthening my ability to communicate,
especially since I had a difficult time in making
sense of my own handwriting. Weight Lifting
was the only activity I took part in. While there

a number of prison uprisings, the two more
publicized were San Quinton and Soledad.

Prison guards were found stabbed to death on a
north yard rec shack. Prisoners were being shot
to death on a San Quinton segregation rec yard,
allegedly attempting to escape with a .25 caliber
automatic hid under a natural wig, smuggled
into the Hole by the prisoners lawyer.

I don't believe there is ever really an absence of fear
with any man. However, I do believe that through time
and experience, a man learns how to master that "fear",
whatever it may be. At the time I had no idea that Life
itself was teaching me in place of my parents or trachers.

The class room had been converted into the
only type of environment capable of getting my
attention long enough where I wanted to be still.

There were a number of times when I found
myself asking the question how I managed to get
myself into the mess and I did know how.

I suppose it was like when Grand-Pa
Jessie killed his Father-ln-Law.

Mister Monroe had already made it clear that he would
kill Jessie if he were to beat his daughter again. The

two got into a disagreement that ended up with Jessie putting hands on her. As a result of that Jessie went looking for his Father-ln-Law, an argument ensued and it cost Jessie five years in Uma State prison.

Jessie was not one to be trifled with. Everyone for miles around knew of his reputation, something I grew to admire and respect about him. He became my role model although I had never met him since he was murdered long before I was born, murdered by men who were afraid of him.

That was the kind of respect I wanted, not what I had watched my own Father put up with and accept from my Mother. I decided respect came from Fear and people needed to have a sense of fearfulness about you in order to respect you. The way I sought to achieve this boundary was by being distant and feeling nothing.

I had no problem with being distant because, from early on I had no sense of what it meant to seriously feel as though I was an actual part of anything. Instead, I taught myself to disguise what was really on my mind and feelings, opposed to waiting to learn what was on the mind of anyone else. I unconsciously developed a distant expression from what I have been told. All nothing more than a protective mechanism

Your first impression is your best impression. Behind prison walls is not a place where upon your very first arriving you want to present yourself as someone who is looking for a friend. Fear is an element with an odor all its own and any evidence of it can cause one to have his back pockets torn off; his Tee Shirt tied in a knot and Kool Aid on his lips for lip stick ending up as somebody's girlfriend.

It has always been my belief that when a person goes to prison and ends up involved in homosexual activities, the tendency has always been there. It makes no difference which role either one is playing pitching or catching. People in prison are a whole different breed of human being. Their life styles almost convert them into a different kind of being that is partially primitive and partially beast like.

Many lose their sense of humanity, that is provided they ever had any to begin with, but the level of morals and principals are nonexistent behind bars. With the exception of the one basic rule of Respect, your life depends on it. Prison life is nothing more than a tiny world within a world. Meaning, everything that goes on out in the streets, go on in a similar way in prison.

Drug Addicts Armed Robbers Rapist. Prisoners actually rob other prisoners. Many actually develop drug habits while in prison and the weak one's partake in activities they ordinarily would not engage in with other men. For me it was like that first time being under the L

Train on Lake Street in Chicago. It was all new to me and! was learning.

Even the choices I made while in prison had an effect on my life along with a number of others long after I had been released back into the free world, I had to play a role in order to get out of prison and I became good at it. These were people with college degrees who are highly paid for their expertise on criminal behavior; people I had to assure that I was no longer a threat to society and I did it.

Aside of instinctively figuring out what I needed to do in order to get out of prison, I had not thought beyond that point of what I would do once I did get out. Going back to what I knew is what got me locked up in the first place. I seriously had no clue as to what to do with my life. The only serious desire I had wad to better myself at being respected and feared. (for all the sense that made)

The only thing I had ever done that I felt was an accomplishment was co-writing a hit record for the late Tyrone Davis, "If I Could Turn Back The Hands Of Time", from which I was not paid one dime since I was on the Lam from certain Agencies at the time and at nineteen years of age my only concern was to avoid a prison stage.

All I did was parlay it.

I spent my time learning how to type, mainly because I for one half the time could not understand my own handwriting, so I figured the best way to

get around that was to learn how to type. Next,
I had to sharpen up my vocabulary because, I
didn't understand half of what the prosecutor was
saying, so every day I would read the dictionary
like a devout Christian would read the Bible.

I knew too that improving the manner in which I spoke
would broaden my prospective of being understood by
the people who were receiving the correspondence.
I started watching the news. Reading the newspaper
keeping up with the changes in the laws and getting a
different prospective of the world from a wider view.

Doing time back in the late 60's through the mid 70's
was nothing but a party. It was like being away at an
all men's college, except the teachers were the Con's
themselves who would share their technique' with
other promising Hustler's to be. There were programs
in which people from the outside could participate.

Acting classes where teachers from Monterey
Peninsula College would come in every Wednesday
night along with numerous other groups that had
the initial interpretation that the classes would
be a part of the rehabilitation process, along
with allowing contact with the outside world
through culture classes, like The Black House.

Racial tension was usually high, but my attitude
was, "It wasn't any of my business, as long as
they stay out of my face". The prison groups like

The B.G.F. Arian Brotherhood The Mexican Mafia kept tension high and the value of life at that time was the cost of a pack of cigarettes.

It wasn't that I was absent of fear, I learned how to master it. I was of the opinion that no one had any reason to address me in any manner for anything, therefore as long as I had no personal interaction with some other prisoner I had no problems. It is amazing how another prisoner knows automatically who not to approach. I kept it that way.

JESSIE

Initially I went to prison too young to know anything about finances or actually functioning in the outside world. Sure I knew how to obtain funds illegally via a variety of criminal avenues, but as far as knowing how to keep it was another story. From the older Cons I learned a number of ways in order to keep "every day money" in my pocket without running the risk of a felony or being shot at by the police.

That too I now look at as strange because each time I was involved in a police chase and shoot-out, I was always laughing. I remember feeling an enormous sense of excitement, almost like I was experiencing the excitement a child experiences when playing a game of hide and seek and suddenly found. No fear, but almost a joyful sensation.

In prison it was only natural for prisoners to gravitate towards their own kind. You had your Bank Robbers Burglars Forgers Pimps Petty Thieves Rapist. Some considered as "Seasoned" in The Game. These were the teachers in The School of Hard Knocks. But the prisoners who were serving time for crimes against women and children were considered the lowest of the low.

All you really have is your name. I had established a reputation as being a good vocalist at Soledad State prison and was asked if I would sing at the first prison wedding in the state of California. That was where I met my first wife who accompanied the bride to be, along with her mother and cousin. I said a total of five words to her: Hello Thank You Good Bye

When we were introduced I said Hello. After my performance she said, Mister I want you to know you can sing at my wedding any time, and I said Thank you. Then when she was leaving I said Good bye. Later on that night her cousin told me she wanted me to write her, but I was not interested, so I never did. The following weekend I was out on the Weight Pile when I hear my name called over the loud speaker for a visit.

One would think that a man in prison serving a ten years to life sentence for armed robbery would not be picky about a woman choosing him, but I was. This woman was not by any means anyone I would think twice about approaching if I were on the bricks, and besides, I already had three other girls who were on my visiting list.

There was this older prisoner. His name was George. He was a few years older that I and we both would practice songs together. It was George who advised me on the reasons why the parole board had just denied me another year. They said I had no responsibilities, as George quickly pointed out, this new woman was the answer to my getting out. She was a supervisor at the post office and was established which was exactly what the parole commission was looking for.

His logic was that it made no difference what she looked like as long as she was able to pay what she weighed. Meaning, prove and show her worth with her actions. This ideal appealed to me. It made sense. Romance without finance is a nuisance.

Shortly after within months after just meeting this woman, she had written a letter to the prison chaplain saying that she had known me before my arrest; that she had been pregnant by me, but lost the baby so she felt it was God's way of letting her know we should be married" Lied to a Priest and I had absolutely no idea she had any intentions of what she was going to do. For me this was nothing more than proving how unscrupulous and low she really was, on top of not being at all appealing. But still, she was going to serve a much needed purpose.

I suppose what I had accomplished in prison caused me to lose sight of the bigger picture. Many of the guys I knew who had gone to prison and got out after serving long stretches of time had nothing and no one to turn to. I on the other hand had managed to acquire a spacious two bedroom home with two car garage my own car and ten fruit trees in the back yard. To me that meant I had beat all odds.

When I paroled to Los Angeles, in 1973, it was my first time ever being there. I was about to start a new life, learning new schemes and ways to extract a pay day out of every day. "Super Stupid" is what I call it. The rage within me would not allow me to see the actual positive part of what I was being given. As far as I was concerned it was all dumb luck

I had no real plans other than learning the streets of LA. At 23, I had no other source of motivation towards anything substantial or constructive within the eyes of the law.

Life was basically just happening. What were opportunities to redirect my life I took as "Breaking Luck". Like the old cliché about Bus Stops.-

If you miss one, another one is coming. My mindset was not geared to function like the average every day American citizen. In my own head I had decided that I had no control over what Life was throwing at me. Sort of like a Crap Shoot except the only thing I chose to gamble with was my life.

To the outside world I appeared fearless and wise, when the truth is I was always uncertain, yet I wasn't afraid which is usually what it took to motivate me into finding myself in high risk and avoidable situations.

Take for instance the copper wire episode. I may have been out of prison six or seven months. I was driving in my car along with an associate who was a mechanic when directly on the corner of the street I lived on, was an open trench left by the telephone company who were installing this huge spool of wire under the ground.

As I turned the corner the mechanic
spoke from the front passenger seat,

"Damn! Look at all that copper
wire." I stop the car and ask,

"You know where to sell it?" he replied,

"Yeah, but first we got to strip all the plastic away"

Without any further delay I step out of the car
removing my suit coat and tell the mechanic to pull the
car down the street in front of my house. I then jump
down in the open ditch and I began to push the two
ton spool of copper wire out of the ditch, up on to the
sidewalk where the spool was so heavy, it left a trail of
cracked concrete all the way to the door of my garage.

Needless to say without going into elaborate
details, the police came knocking, but I managed
to give them the slip for the next two years and
not once did I ever consider apprehension. In
my mind I was the smoothest thing since Satin.
Yet at the same time dumb as a box of bricks.

Between 1973 and 1978, life for me was whatever
opportunity that happened to come along. I had
become enlightened to numerous other hustles over
the years so I was virtually living my life like a shark

in the water where I had to keep moving or else I would die; living purely off instincts, which is fine for a fish, but as a human being direction is required in order to exist in this world among other people.

Emotionally I was unattached, yet within that first year after being released from Soledad, I was entertaining three additional women from the Los Angeles area, not including the woman I married in prison. The cocaine use happened almost accidently. I did not indulge in snorting blow because I did not like the method up my nose. But when I walked in on the mechanic at his home, I thought he was shooting Heroin, but once he had shown me it was cocaine and I had one taste, that was it for me. For the following Eighteen months I would inject Cocaine four to five times a day every day.

The three habits I knew that Jessie had were Drinking Gambling and his Philandering. The one trait I did not have was the gambling, but the other two must have been in my blood.

On a fluke I was arrested in Oakland and ultimately charged with parole violation. Ended up being given six months and I requested to be sent to San Quinton because it was in the San Francisco Bay Area. Through release programs I was sent to a halfway house on Grove Street in Oakland, where I knew virtually everybody.

Cocaine back then was considered as "The champagne of narcotics, but you had to have money to have it".

As I would inform people that I no longer indulged, clearly they all thought I was being modest and would give me ridiculous amounts of Blow for free. Then when I would run into that person sometime later and they'd ask how the Blow was. My reply would be that I sold it. After a while it turned into something else.

The drugs gave me a false sense of power; superiority and confidence, yet I realized the consequences were not something that I chose to contend with. I don't consider myself as really anything, but one thing I am Not is Weak.

Once again I knew what I didn't want, but had no idea of what I did want or how I planned to get it. Like an empty row boat out on the Ocean in choppy water. At no time did I ever consider the future because, inside I had a Death Wish just like Jessie.

AND ME

By

Donald D Conley Sr.

AND ME

Thirty-Nine more until 100, not that I have any
intention or hopes of ever getting anywhere that
number in age, but I am now at a point in my life where
what once mattered no longer has the same luster as it
did when I was younger. Woodrow Wilson once said,

"We grow by our dreams". Okay, I ask myself what
dreams do I have at this late stage of my life. Although
it's only "too late" when you're under the ground.,
but for the most part any dreams or aspirations I may
have had, I can only hope to convey the positive

When I was first released from federal prison, I spent a
considerable amount of time in Baldwin Hills, (a.k.a.)
The Jungle on the street where the movie Training Day
was filmed. The Blood's occupied that section of Los
Angeles and their color was Red. At that time I drove a
diplomat Blue silver pinstripe Cadillac Coupe De Ville.

The first time I met Bone, who was a
character in the movie Training

Day he commented on the my car
with what I took as scarcasm,

"That's a mean ride. Only thing is it's the wrong
color" was what he said and I replied,

"That's why it belongs to me cause it ain't for
everybody to like" looking straight into his eyes
while the other three guys with him appeared to
be waiting with bated breath for a reaction. It was a
warm summer day and I wore only a "Wife Beater"
with some slacks and loafers. I still kept most of my
muscularity, from which the topic went until I was
invited to come to the last apartment building on
Pinafore close to the park where an entire weight
training gym, mirrors included was set up.

As it turned out for a while the weight room was
jumping. Sometimes there would be three and
four teams two people per team all working out at
the same time, but on different body parts. At no
time did I ever claim to be affiliated, but I was best
considered as the OG with mad bodybuilding skills.

The last time I saw Bone was on the news when
Shugg Knight killed Terry Carter in the Tam's
parking lot on Central and Rosecrans with his
truck. Bone was with Terry, Shugg was just scary.

One thing I can say with certainty, if you live long enough and are paying attention to what is going on around you. A great many things will become clear once you learn how to quiet yourself. One main fear of people in prison is being sent to the Hole, which means being alone. For me the Hole was an ideal place to be. I have always said that I am my best company when left alone.

Instinctively I understood the mentality of gangs. Like a pack of wild wolves who follow the Alfa Male. Get the leader, you got the Crew. The point Had I shown a glimmer of uncertainty events to follow from that day forward would have been bloody.

During that time I was on federal parole on the run, but still in Los

Angeles working a square job driving truck for a Stationary company. While on the run, I was buying a home in Compton, had my own work truck and a customized Cadillac Coupe De Ville. When arrested and ultimately charged with parole violation, I had made preparations to prove my position about the parole agent deliberately trying to goad me back into federal prison. As a direct result of my actions, the parole commission ruled against the parole agent and ordered that I be released immediately.

Needless to say, the clown was as hot as fish grease when he got the news from the parole commission that they would not abide by his recommendation to return me to custody. I would go to his office with a tape recorder, which I placed directly on his desk and played for him to hear, but instead of hitting the off button, I accidently hit the record button and recorded every word he said. I made a copy of the tape and mailed it to the parole commission in Washington, D.C. Three times I did this, but he was too arrogant to even think he was playing himself with his own authority.

When news of that got out, many parolees started carrying tape recorders with them until the parole office made a rule of no devices with recording ability allowed. (A clear sign that something is wrong within the agency that they don't want known publicly.) The agents are the major part of the high recidivism rate in prisons to this day, a fact that contributes to Modern Day Slavery. At some point I stopped being a part of the problem and became aware.

There I was, in the bowels of the federal penitentiary cursing out a federal parole commissioner and ended up getting a parole date after being denied ten years.

Between reading the law books and not being afraid to challenge the federal government, I was able to rise above what was expected to be a very dyer situation for me. Instead it became a learning experience, one that I could not have obtained anywhere else on earth. I took pride in being able to maintain my integrity when virtually everyone else seem to bow down and simply accept what they were told.

Life is 10% of what happens to me and 90% of how I react to it. A fact that only time has proven along with teaching a rather tumultuous lesson filled with events and lessons to live by. If History has taught us anything, we know that it is doomed to repeat itself. Therefore, as "Tontoe" said to the Lone Ranger in Blazing Sadles,

"Kemosabe, in order to endure we must persevere."

The strongest principal of Growth is Human Choice. It is within these choices we make which form our character morals and ideals that will ultimately carry us through life or end it for us in death. However, the bottom line is that everything in this life starts First with you.

I doubt I will ever look back on my life and wonder how much better it could have been. I am not a wishful thinker. Beings are the Owners of their own actions good or bad. No one is able to go back in time and re-live the past, but at any time anyone can create a new beginning.

ANY DAY NOW

Printed in the United States
By Bookmasters